The Astral Legacies Tigers' Secret

Written by Gordon Volke

This edition published in Great Britain in 2009 by Quest, an imprint of Top That! Publishing plc,
Marine House, Tide Mill Way, Woodbridge, Suffolk, IP12 1AP, UK
www.quest-books.co.uk
0 2 4 6 8 9 7 5 3 1

Editorial Director – Daniel Graham
Creative Director – Simon Couchman
Art Editor – Matt Denny
Website Design – Paul Strandoo

Written by Gordon Volke

ISBN 978-1-84666-851-7

A catalogue record for this book is available from the British Library
Printed and bound in China

The Astral Legacies
Tigers' Secret

Written by Gordon Volke

Connor·R
is my Best
Buddy

Quest

Published by Quest.
Quest is an imprint of Top That! Publishing plc,
Tide Mill Way, Woodbridge, Suffolk, IP12 1AP, UK
www.quest-books.co.uk

How the book works ...

Join Asha in her quest to find the second Astral Legacy by searching for the hidden locations online. At key points in the book, the tigers provide Asha with precise information relating to the destinations that she must visit in order to complete her quest. Each GPS (Global Positioning System) coordinate that is transmitted by the tigers represents a precise location in Asia.

By entering the GPS coordinates into the GeoLocator function on **www.astrallegacies.com**, you will be able to travel with Asha on her quest. Click the tiger icon on the revolving carousel, then select the 'GeoLocator' link to begin. For example, try these coordinates – they will take you to the Burj Dubai in Dubai:

25°11'49.07" N,
55°16'26.55" E

When you 'arrive' at each new destination online, you will discover the famous landmark that Asha is seeking.

Enter GPS code here

Select compass direction here

Use this slider to zoom in and see the location in more detail

Explore the area in more detail by clicking here

Click on the red arrow to reveal the location

As the adventure unfolds, keep a note of the locations that you find. When you have identified all ten key locations that Asha visits on her quest, enter the words that make up each location into the 'wordsearch' grid at the back of this book. If you have ringed the correct words, the location of the second Astral Legacy will be revealed from the unused letters in the grid.

Log-on to **www.astrallegacies.com** to report the location of the second Astral Legacy. If you successfully enter this final landmark, the quest is complete and you will be able to read the thrilling climax to *Tigers' Secret*.

T	A	J	K	R	E	G	I	S	T	A	N
A	V	R	T	S	E	R	E	V	E	C	A
E	E	L	E	R	A	N	I	M	E	E	T
R	S	E	A	M	L	L	L	D	I	N	S
G	O	C	N	D	A	A	A	R	M	T	I
O	U	A	U	R	I	R	Y	H	N	R	K
T	A	L	H	R	T	V	E	U	A	E	A
E	R	A	E	D	L	I	O	D	L	M	P
I	E	P	L	E	S	M	C	S	L	O	C
K	M	R	E	K	R	A	K	A	T	A	U
I	O	G	N	O	I	T	A	T	S	O	G
W	A	L	L	O	F	C	H	I	N	A	K

Once you have completed the wordsearch, the unused letters spell out the location of the second Astral Legacy.

Important Hints & Tips

• Enter the GPS coordinates accurately, including the compass direction.

• Use the 'Notes' section at the back of this book to record the locations that you identify as you progress through the quest. You will then have everything at hand to complete the 'wordsearch' puzzle at the end of the book and finish the quest with Asha.

• The tigers have provided additional clues to help you fill in the wordsearch correctly at the back of this book.

Chapter 1

An Ambush of Tigers

Sixteen-year-old Asha Ghosh was exceptional for her age. Despite never going to school, she had learned to read and write, mainly thanks to her late father who, even after an exhausting day pulling his rickshaw around the streets of Kolkata (Calcutta), had always found time to teach her. Asha was also a wonderful cook – although her meagre wages meant that she barely had enough money to buy food, she had a natural flair for using herbs and spices, some of which she haggled for at the local market and others which she grew outside the tumbledown shack in the rural Indian village where she lived with her sick mother and two little brothers, Dabeet and Madhuk. Asha also had a brilliant memory. Tell her something once and she would never forget it. Show her something once and she would be able to do it immediately. Her mother said she was like an elephant, but that is where the comparison ended. Asha was light and agile … and as thin as a rake!

Asha's village was about three and a half miles from the outskirts of Kolkata. Every morning at sunrise and every evening at sunset, Asha had to make the long trek through the dusty, parched Indian countryside to and from Nazir Kapoor's clothing factory where she had worked since she was five. She sewed sports clothes that were sold in Europe and America for twenty or thirty times what they had cost to make. Not many in the West cared that the smart shirts and fashionable shorts with their all-important brand logos were turned out, hour after hour, in a dirty overcrowded sweatshop by what amounted to slave labour. It was simply the laws of economics, the way of the world.

Once, when she was about twelve, Asha had joined one of the city's many trade unions in the hope of securing a fairer wage for all those hours of mind-numbing toil. It proved to be a big mistake.

Nazir Kapoor, the factory owner, now regarded her as a troublemaker and his cruel supervisor, Dhalia Menokki took every opportunity to bully and torment her. Asha lived a life of constant work and worry. Yet she always remained cheerful and had a kind word for everyone. The bosses may distrust her, but her friends and fellow workers did not. Asha's steadfast cheerfulness, despite her hard life ensured that she was very popular and was loved by everyone.

One night, on her way back to the village after another fourteen-hour shift, Asha startled when she thought she saw a female Bengal tiger slinking through some nearby trees. It appeared to be following her.

'I've been sewing for too long in bad light,' she said to herself. 'My eyes are playing tricks on me.'

But, that night, the sighting was enough to make Asha dream about tigers as she lay in her narrow bed with her mother coughing in her sleep beside her. It was a particularly vivid dream and one that

Asha found totally convincing. In the dream, the tiger approached the shack and began talking to her through some kind of weird mental telepathy. The tiger spoke straight into Asha's mind, telling her an amazing story ...

About 50,000 years ago, a race of aliens visited Earth with a view to colonising it. They travelled in a spacecraft powered by the 'Vortex of Light,' a triangular prism created by a hologram and containing seven objects from different parts of the solar system, each one a different colour of the rainbow. The prism generated enough energy to allow the aliens to travel anywhere in the universe at the speed of light.

At first, the aliens were pleased with their choice of colony. Earth was a beautiful, unspoilt place with lots of habitable land, wildlife and natural resources. The only humans were tribes of hunter-gatherers, living in harmony with nature. Tragically, soon after the aliens' arrival in what is now the Arizona Desert in North America, a natural disaster devastated their peaceful colonisation. A meteor struck Earth right beside them and obliterated their spacecraft. The precious items from the 'Vortex of Light' were sucked up into the atmosphere by the impact debris and carried around the world where they eventually fell to Earth and were lost. The aliens not killed by the strike spent the rest of their lives searching for their missing astral objects and instructing all the animal species they met to do the same. As the survivors died, their bodies instantly evaporated and left no trace of their existence.

Now a new generation of aliens had returned to Earth to reclaim their seven items which, having been left for so long, had now been named The Astral Legacies. On arrival, they were horrified to find how much the planet had changed in such a comparatively short space of time. Humans had spread around the world and their impact on the environment was catastrophic – habitats destroyed, animals extinct, widespread pollution and increasing global warming. Having heard stories from their ancestors about how idyllic Earth was before, the aliens wanted to reverse this trend by exterminating the whole of the human race, but the wiser heads among them pointed out that such a punishment would be unfair. It was the older generation of human beings that were responsible for these terrible crimes – the young are innocent. So an agreement was reached.

The aliens will leave Earth alone, provided their seven Astral Legacies are returned. Seven young people, chosen at random, will be given the task of finding them within a single calendar year. If they succeed, the human race will be spared in the hope that this new generation can reverse the damage done by their elders. If the young people fail in any respect, humankind will be wiped out in a stroke …

At this point, Asha woke up. She sat bolt upright in bed with a shriek, startling her mother, which set off another bad bout of coughing.

'Oh, my goodness! We've overslept, Treacle,'

spluttered her mother. 'Get up now or you will be late for work.'

(Treacle was Asha's pet name within the family, relating to an incident when she was very little and had eaten a whole tin with a spoon.) But Asha was still transfixed by her dream. Over breakfast, despite her mother's repeated reminders about the time, Asha began to relate her incredible story … only to find Madhuk mimicking her by holding up his old soft-toy tiger and pretending to make it speak while Dabeet rolled on the floor, helpless with laughter.

Chuckling herself at the ridiculous nature of what she was saying, Asha hurried out into the hazy, early morning light to begin her long walk to the factory.

Then, as she was walking through an area of deserted woodland with a narrow path running through it, three big tigers surrounded Asha. To see one tiger so close to a major city was most unusual; to see a group of them together (known as an 'ambush' of tigers) was very rare indeed. In fact, it was so astonishing that Asha forgot to be frightened.

'Greetings, Asha,' said the first tiger, speaking directly into her mind in the same manner as in her dream.

'We will not harm you. We need to talk to you urgently. You are our Chosen One.'

Then a second tiger stepped forwards, a magnificent fully grown male with vivid orange and black stripes and a pure white tummy. He was obviously the leader of the group, the dominant male, who spoke to Asha in a way that made it clear he was used to being obeyed.

'Do you remember the dream you had last night?' he asked.

'Indeed I do,' replied the girl, eagerly. 'It was incredible ...'

'Please, Asha,' interrupted the tiger. 'Do not delay us with your idle chatter. It is incredibly dangerous for us to be here like this. We are hunted by your cruel species to make your ridiculous clothes, your disgusting medicines and for your so-called sport. That means we cannot stay in any one place for very long. But we must speak to you on a matter of the utmost urgency. The story relayed to you in the dream is true. The first Astral Legacy has been found. Now the search begins for the second one. We are the guardians of this precious object. You have been chosen to find it.'

At first, the enormity of these words did not sink in to Asha's confused, racing brain. When they did, she collapsed on the spot like a pack of cards! She was soon back on her feet again, however, after a huge, rough tongue had licked her face and another big wet nose had gently nuzzled her upwards.

'You are right to be overwhelmed with the size and importance of your task,' continued the leader of the tigers. 'The future of humankind rests upon your shoulders. But we are confident you can do this, Asha. Even in your short life, you have shown yourself to be like us – quick, fearless and strong – and so we have chosen you to find the second Astral Legacy. Do not think of your task as an ordeal, think of it as an honour. Not many girls of your age have the strength of character required to complete the quest.'

At this point, the third tiger (the female that Asha had seen stalking her the day before) gave a low warning growl.

'We must leave now,' said the dominant male tiger, urgently. 'People are coming, they must not see us.'

'Oh, please don't go yet,' begged Asha. 'I don't understand this task. How do I go about finding the second Astral Legacy?'

'Listen carefully and I will tell you,' replied the dominant male tiger, quickly. 'We know where the object is hidden and you must find it in the way decided by our alien masters. Soon, we shall stop talking to you directly. Instead, we will telepathically command your hand to write down ten sets of GPS coordinates, each one pinpointing a different place in Asia. You must use the coordinates to discover where each place is, write down its name and then visit it in person. When you have visited all ten places, we will advise you how to use the names to discover exactly where the second Astral Legacy is hidden.'

'Why can't you just give me the coordinates of the hiding place and I can go straight there?' asked Asha.

'Because,' purred the tiger, pleased by the girl's quick thinking and no-nonsense logic, 'this is a test! Our masters, the aliens, want to be sure the human race is worth saving. So it is down to you and the other chosen children to show how brave and determined humans can be.'

Pausing only to remind Asha that her task must be completed as quickly as possible and with absolute secrecy, the tigers turned and began to disappear through the trees like silent ghosts. Suddenly, Asha felt a rush of panic as she realised she did not have the means to undertake her task.

'How do I pay for this trip?' she called. 'I have no money to travel around Asia.'

The third tiger stopped and turned her head.

'An opportunity will be offered to you, Asha,' she explained. 'You must recognise it when it comes and be bold enough to take it. Otherwise, all will be lost.'

With that, the creature departed, leaving Asha feeling wildly excited and completely terrified at the same time.

Chapter 2

Two Princesses

'You're fired!' snarled Nazir Kapoor, the factory owner, as Asha rushed into the factory and sat down at her sewing machine.

'But I'm only twenty minutes late, sir,' Asha replied, looking as meek and sorry as possible.

'An hour, more like!' yelled the angry owner. 'You know the rules, Ghosh. Persistent lateness means instant dismissal.'

'But I haven't been late for ages, sir ...' protested Asha.

'Don't argue with me, girl!' shouted Nazir Kapoor, furiously. 'What kept you, anyway? Was it your poor old sick mother ... again?'

Asha opened her mouth to say she had been delayed by a trio of Bengal tigers, but she promptly closed it when she realised how laughable that would sound.

'Yes, sir,' she answered, timidly.

The glare on the man's smooth-shaven face told Asha he really meant to sack her this time, but she was saved by the intervention of Dhalia Menokki, the factory supervisor, or so it seemed. Dhalia knew Asha's worth as a worker and did not want to lose her. At the same time, the cunning woman saw an opportunity to turn this situation to their advantage.

'Excuse me, sir,' she interrupted, smiling with her mouth but not with her cold, hard eyes. 'May I suggest we give this tiresome girl one last chance ... provided she agrees to certain terms and conditions?'

'And what might they be?' enquired Nazir Kapoor, sensing something interesting was coming.

'Miss Ghosh may keep her job provided she works a 16-hour day for the next seven days on half-pay.'

'That's outrageous!' exclaimed Asha.

'Take it or leave it, my dear,' said Nazir Kapoor

with an evil grin.

Asha hesitated. She knew she was being further exploited, but a few rupees was better than none at all and her family would surely starve if she had no work.

'I accept,' she whispered.

'Pardon?' said Dhalia Menokki, deliberately making Asha say it again to humiliate her further.

'I said, I accept!' repeated Asha in an over-loud voice.

'Splendid!' chuckled Nazir Kapoor, turning away and rubbing his hands together with satisfaction. 'Well done, Ms Menokki. Keep up the good work!'

Sitting at her machine for two-thirds of every day meant Asha had no time to make the long walk to and from her village. So she slept in the factory, curled up on a dirty mat in the corner like an animal. She barely ate anything, sending her tiny wage home to her family via one of the other workers. She had only completed three days of this ordeal, but already it felt like a lifetime.

On the fourth night, after a particularly tedious day, Asha could not bear to be in the factory for a moment longer. She had to get out for some fresh air. Knowing she was losing precious sleeping time that she would bitterly regret in the morning, she crept out of the stifling building and went for a walk in the cool darkness of night.

Strolling into the wealthy part of the city, Asha headed for a small, well-kept park just across the road from Nazir Kapoor's splendid town house. Sitting down on a wooden bench, the weary teenager looked up at the moon as it came out from behind a cloud. She felt burdened with responsibility – her work, her family and, above all, her quest, which seemed no nearer to beginning. How many other people, she wondered, were looking up at the same moon at this moment without a care in the world?

Suddenly, her thoughts were interrupted by the sound of someone sobbing. It was a heart-wrenching sound, the crying of someone deeply unhappy, and Asha felt motivated to try and help, despite all of her own urgent problems. Looking around, she spotted a girl of about her own age sitting on another bench, rocking backwards and forwards with her face buried in her hands. Asha went over and sat down beside the wailing teenager, putting a comforting arm round her shoulder. Immediately, the girl turned to her for a cuddle, like a little child, even though she had no idea who Asha was or what she was doing there.

The young woman clung on for a long time until she realised what she was doing and broke away.

'I'm sorry,' she said.

Looking at the girl's face for the first time, Asha was struck by the similarity to her own. They both had smooth brown skin, bright blue eyes and long black hair that reached down to their shoulders at the back. Then, when the girl stood up to go, Asha was further struck by her figure. It was also just like her own! Asha's poverty made her painfully thin; clearly, this girl did not eat through unhappiness.

The likeness between the two of them was uncanny. They looked just like identical twins! Was this just by chance or did it have some deeper purpose?

As the other girl turned to leave, Asha asked her 'double' why she was so deeply unhappy. The girl was more than willing to talk about herself and her terrible sorrow. What she said took Asha by surprise, though she did not show it.

'My name is Corinne Kapoor,' explained the tear-stained teenager. 'I am the daughter of Nazir Kapoor, the factory owner.'

'I work for him,' chipped in Asha.

'Then you know what he is like!' exclaimed Corinne, bitterly. 'Mean, cruel and domineering. He must always have his own way. Especially about me!'

'What about you?' probed Asha, gently.

'About my marriage to Narmal Vazkar!' cried the girl, indignantly. 'I am being forced to marry a man over twice my age whom I have not even met!'

Corinne went on to explain that her husband-to-be was a business associate of her father. Narmal Vazkar owned a factory in Mumbai that supplied the material from which Nazir Kapoor made his sports clothes. The men's plan was to merge their two businesses into one family firm by way of this marriage. Corinne's feelings did not enter into it. She was just a pawn in their cunning, money-making game. The trouble was that the girl already had a true love called Devesh. He was the son of her father's gardener. They had played together as children and became sweethearts when they were teenagers. Now both seventeen, they lived only for each other and were planning to get married themselves as soon as they possibly could.

'I cannot wed anyone except Devesh!' exclaimed Corinne, bursting into tears again. 'He is my other half. My soulmate. We *have* to be together for the rest of our lives.'

After this, the two girls sat in silence for a very long time. Then, as if emerging from a dream, Corinne also noticed that she was sitting next to someone who looked the image of herself. Her eyes flared wide open as a wild idea came into her head.

'What is it, Corinne?' asked Asha.

'Nothing,' replied the other girl, hurriedly.

'Go on, tell me,' urged Asha. 'I promise I'll listen, whatever it is.'

'Well …' began Corinne, hesitantly. 'I've just noticed how alike we are … and that has given me a crazy idea. Supposing … no, it is too silly! Please forget it!'

'You can't leave it there, Corinne!' cried Asha in frustration. 'What's on your mind? Tell me!'

'Well,' continued the girl, with rising excitement in her voice, 'Supposing … just supposing … we changed places, you know, completely swapped identities. You became me and I became you. Then I would be an unknown factory girl free to elope with my true love and marry him in secret. You could get away from my father … as a wealthy society girl you could take a sightseeing tour of India and the surrounding countries in Asia.'

Suddenly, Asha realised this was the chance that the tigers had told her she would be given. Daunting and dangerous though it sounded, she knew that she had to take it. But there was something she had to clear up first.

'You do realise you'll be giving up all your wealth and status,' explained Asha.

'I don't care about that!' replied Corinne, passionately. 'What happiness have these things ever brought me? None whatsoever! But if you agree to this swap, you will be giving me freedom and love – and they are utterly priceless!'

Having agreed on their plan, the girls shook hands and arranged to meet back at the park at midnight in three days' time, at the end of Asha's week of forced labour. They promised to bring suitable clothes for each other to wear. Corinne also said she would bring her passport, international credit card and other items that Asha would need to go travelling.

'What's brilliant, Corinne,' added Asha, as they

stood together at the park gates, 'is when you go missing, your father will come looking for me, thinking I am you. His problem will be that he won't know where I've gone – and there'll be no way for him to find out, either!'

Giggling excitedly, the girls parted company, with Asha not realising how wrong she would turn out to be!

The remaining days of work went by in a flash. Instead of looking at the clock all the time, as she usually did, Asha was absorbed in her own thoughts, planning how she should organise her trip to other countries in search of the second Astral Legacy. Her one worry was that she did not know where to start. The tigers had not been in touch with her again to complete the briefing of her mission.

Three days later, Corinne was waiting impatiently for her by the front gates of the park as Asha arrived on the stroke of midnight as arranged. The tired factory girl had just managed to run home to collect some old clothes and stuff them into a carrier bag, which she exchanged for a smart suitcase full of expensive Western-style outfits and all the other items that she needed.

'Are you quite sure about this?' asked Asha.

'I've never been more sure of anything in my life,' replied Corinne. 'My father has always called me princess, but I've never felt like one. But now that I'm free to marry my prince, I do!'

'I feel like a princess, too,' laughed Asha, taking some pretty shoes and a state-of-the-art mobile phone out of the suitcase.

'This will add to your makeover,' chuckled Corinne, taking a big diamond ring off her finger and handing it to Asha. 'This ring is said to bring good luck to the wearer once in her lifetime. My luck has been in meeting you. So you must have it now and renew the promise of luck for yourself.'

Argument would mean delay, so Asha pushed the ring onto her finger, embraced Corinne and picked up her suitcase. Then the two girls disappeared in opposite directions into the night, each returning home to spend their last night as their true selves.

The tigers contacted Asha on her way home to the village in the small hours of the following morning. Two males were waiting for her in the same piece of wooded ground they had used before.

'Where's the female?' asked Asha.

'Shot!' answered the leader, curtly. 'If the human race is finally spared, your new generation might stop this senseless slaughter ... but there is no time to discuss the matter now. We've come to say goodbye to you, Asha, and wish you good luck. From now on, we will only communicate with you like this ...'

The tiger squinted his beautiful eyes and Asha felt a tremor beginning in her right hand, urging her to write something down. Searching through the suitcase given to her by Corinne, she found a leather-bound diary and a jewel-encrusted pen that she used to scribble down the following sequence of letters, numbers and symbols ...

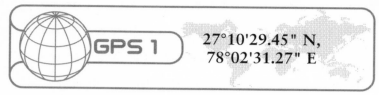

GPS 1 — 27°10'29.45" N, 78°02'31.27" E

'Are these the GPS coordinates of the first place I have to visit?' asked Asha, looking up from her book. But the tigers were gone! They had melted away through the trees while she was writing, leaving the girl feeling very alone. As usual, however, she looked on the positive side.

'Come on, Asha,' she said to herself. 'Travelling abroad at someone else's expense has got to be better than sewing sports clothes, even if the future of humankind is at stake!'

Chapter 3

One Teardrop
Upon the Cheek of Time

Asha had never been on a train before. She knew nothing about reading destination boards or buying tickets, but she learned from watching others. When she was ready, she queued up and asked for a ticket to Agra, paying for it with Corinne's credit card as smoothly and effortlessly as if she had done it all her life. Then she took her seat in the carriage, looking out of the window at the pantomime of porters and travellers rushing backwards and forwards with piles of luggage. Asha herself was travelling light. She had ditched the expensive suitcase in favour of her old rucksack into which she had packed everything she needed – a change of clothes, the credit card, the diary and pen and the mobile phone she had just learned to use.

It had been a long night for Asha with very little

sleep. Arriving home at 3 am, after her final meeting with the tigers, the teenager had taken most of the cash out of Corinne's purse and left it beside her fitfully-sleeping mother with a brief note of explanation. Asha just said she had to go away for a while and this money was to help the family while she was gone. Then she had to sort out her belongings and make sure she did not forget anything, a task made more difficult by her mother's frequent bouts of coughing that kept threatening to wake her up. The hardest part had been saying goodbye to her two little brothers. Fast asleep in their beds, they looked like little angels instead of the mischievous rascals they really were. Asha felt a tear or two rolling down her cheeks as she realised she would not see them again for several weeks – or maybe never again!

Finally, as an old cockerel began to crow, Asha slipped out of the house and hurried away from the village just as she had done so many times in the past ten years. This time, though, she was not heading for the hated clothing factory. She was on her way to Kolkata station to begin the greatest adventure of her life. She felt a mixture of fear and elation and by the time she had completed the long walk in from the countryside, she felt tired, too. With the little cash she had kept for herself, she bought some coffee and samosas for breakfast and then, having two or three hours to wait for her train, she allowed herself the luxury of a little sleep – once she had mastered Corinne's mobile phone functions.

A little boy sitting next to her on a station bench had shown her how to switch it on and off. He also wanted to demonstrate how to ring one of the numbers in the memory, but that would have been dangerous, so she declined.

On her own and by a process of trial and error, she discovered how to use the phone's GPS facility, entering the first coordinates the tigers had given her over and over again until she understood how to make them bring up full details of the place to which they referred. Once she understood this routine, the teenager felt confident that she would be able to pinpoint anywhere in Asia simply by entering the different sequences of numbers and letters into the satellite mapping website facility on the phone.

Now, at last, she was safely on board the train and the guard was blowing his shrill whistle, sending her on the long journey across the heart of India from Kolkata in the east to Agra in the north. This ancient city was the capital of the famous Mughal emperors and site of one of the most beautiful buildings in the world. Asha had always wanted to see it. Now she would get the chance.

Gazing at the Indian countryside flashing past her window with its familiar collage of heat-scorched grass, straggling villages, donkeys plodding along the dusty roads and half-naked children stopping their games to wave at the train, the young teenager felt happy and contented. It was indeed an honour that she, Asha Ghosh, had been selected for this task.

'Hello, Corinne!' exclaimed a gushing voice.

Continuing to stare out of the window, Asha started, remembering she was meant to be Corinne. Looking around, she found herself staring at a girl wearing expensive-looking clothes who plonked herself down on an empty seat opposite.

'Fancy meeting you,' continued the stranger, excitedly. 'Are you also using half-term week to go sightseeing?'

'Something like that,' murmured Asha.

'I'm going to text Gatita,' chuckled the girl, taking out her mobile phone. 'Hi, it's Ranjana. Just met classmate Corinne on the train!'

'Don't bother,' said Asha, quickly. 'It's hardly newsworthy.'

Feeling panic-stricken inside but showing no outward trace of emotion, Asha realised she would have to do some brilliant acting if her true identity was to remain a secret. So she adopted the strategy of letting her companion do most of the talking (something she was clearly happy to do) and just nod and laugh at the appropriate places. In the end, the tedious conversation about parents and teachers and boys that Asha did not know petered out and Ranjana settled back with her magazine, leaving her imagined classmate to pretend to go to sleep.

So far, so good, thought Asha, gleefully. She hasn't seen through me yet and it's only another hour and a half before we get there.

Murmuring something about needing to get somewhere in a hurry, Asha left Ranjana as the train pulled into Agra station. She nudged her way down the crowded corridor and got off the moment the train stopped, its brakes emitting a single loud hiss as if sighing with satisfaction at completing the journey. Hurrying away through the throngs of people milling around on the platform, Asha imagined she would never meet Ranjana again in her lifetime.

The beauty of the white marble mausoleum that was Asha's first destination took her breath away. It was everything she imagined … and more! Looking down the long approach to the building, the exquisite dome with its bronze spire pointing upwards at the sky shone brightly in the late afternoon sunshine. The smaller domes and the minaret towers on either side of the approach gave the scene a perfect symmetry, pleasing the eye in every respect. Yet, for all its beauty, there was an air of sadness about this place. It was, after all, a tomb.

Built for one woman, Mumtaz Mahal, beloved wife of Mughal Emperor Shah Jahan … she read in her guide book. Then she saw a line by the Kolkata-born poet, Rabi Tagore, whose famous poems and stories she had once shared with her father. He described the building as 'one teardrop upon the cheek of time.' This summed up Asha's feelings about it perfectly.

Having visited the first location given to her by the tigers successfully, Asha was beginning to wonder what would happen next when she felt the insistent shaking starting up again in her right hand. Grabbing the diary and pen from her rucksack, she scribbled down the next set of coordinates dictated to her by the tigers ...

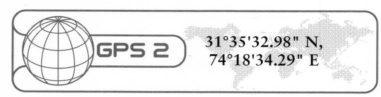

GPS 2

31°35'32.98" N, 74°18'34.29" E

Feeling elated that her quest was going so well, Asha turned around and started to leave ... only to walk straight into Ranjana again!

'Fancy meeting you here!' exclaimed the other girl, clearly annoyed at being left on the train in such a rude manner. 'What happened to you, then? Get the runs?'

'I told you, Ranjana,' replied Asha, deciding attack was the best form of defence. 'I needed to get here in a hurry.'

'Why?' persisted the other girl.

'Oh, nothing important,' replied Asha, casually.

'Either you're meeting a secret lover or you're

trying to avoid me. So which one is it, Corinne?'
demanded Ranjana.

'Neither!' exclaimed Asha, giving a big smile and
trying to laugh off the other girl's rising annoyance.
'Don't be cross, Rani. I thought you were my
buddy!'

Clearly delighted at being called by her short
name and included in Corinne's circle of friends,
Ranjana beamed from ear to ear and whipped out
her mobile phone.

'Stand there, in front of the building,' she said.
'I'm going to take a photo of you.'

'There's no need ...' called Asha.

'I insist!' cried Ranjana, taking the photograph.
'Now you take one of me and then we'll ask a
passer-by to take one of us together.'

Asha went along with this plan, not daring to
dash away again for fear of arousing the other girl's
suspicions.

In fact, a few moments later, the whole
unwelcome encounter turned into a nightmare for

Asha. Ranjana held her mobile phone aloft to get a good signal and started to feverishly press some of the buttons.

'What are you doing now?' asked Asha.

'Sending these pictures to my parents,' said Ranjana, excitedly. 'Being your father's bank manager, my dad is very close to your dad and our families will enjoy seeing us having a good time together.'

Before Asha could stop her, the images were winging their way through cyberspace. Now Nazir Kapoor would know exactly where she was! Her cover was blown! It would only be a matter of time before he tried to catch up with her and drag her back to Kolkata. As far as the factory owner would be concerned, Asha was his runaway daughter and the sooner he returned her for marriage to Narmal Vazkar, the better.

Asha left the World Heritage Site with a heavy heart.

'Don't tell me you're off again?' asked Ranjana,

hurrying after her. 'We haven't looked inside the building yet.'

'Sorry, I have to go,' muttered Asha.

'You *do* have a secret lover, don't you?' whooped Ranjana, almost beside herself with excitement. 'What's his name? Is he handsome? Where are you meeting him?'

Asha ran off, not bothering to answer any of the questions.

'Can I text Gatita?' called the girl, waving her mobile around again. 'Will that get you into trouble?'

'You've done that already!' said Asha through clenched teeth.

Chapter 4

The Wrath of the Dragon

Before she left India, Asha made sure she had a full stomach. She had hardly eaten anything for the past few days and, on occasions, had been feeling faint and light-headed. So she found herself a small restaurant near Delhi station and ordered herself a feast fit for a queen. She began with potato and cauliflower pakoras, crispy bite-size pieces of vegetables deep-fried in hot oil. They were delicious served with a side salad and mint-flavoured yoghurt sauce. For her main course she had tandoori chicken and naan bread, a speciality of this region of northern India. Nibbling the succulent, red-coloured chicken cooked in a special clay oven, she read on the menu that this dish had delighted Pandit Nehru, the first Prime Minister of India, as well as visiting American Presidents John F Kennedy and Richard Nixon. She felt in exalted company! Then she finished her meal with gulab jamun, little balls of rich dough flavoured with cardamom seeds and rose water, swimming in sugar syrup. As she left the restaurant, she felt ready to take on the world!

Asha had travelled the comparatively short distance from Agra to Delhi on a local train, fearful of running into Ranjana again if she used the express. It was a long, hot and crowded journey with frequent stops and starts. The teenager had opted to wear casual Western clothes, a designer T-shirt and a pair of jeans, on the grounds that it would make her look like a tourist. But on this train full of poverty-stricken men and women with crying babies, it made her look rich and privileged. She could see it in the dull stares that everyone gave her. What are you doing here? said their looks. You don't belong!

Asha longed to tell them she was just a simple factory girl. But she knew it was pointless … and dangerous. So she endured their quiet hostility until the old wooden train finally rattled into the country's capital city.

Spending the night in a hotel and catching a taxi to Delhi's International Airport early the following morning, the teenager boarded a flight to Pakistan, using Corinne's credit card to pay for everything. This was the first time Asha had been on an aeroplane and she expected to feel a bit nervous, but in fact she loved every minute of it. The scream of the engines as the plane thundered down the runway and lifted into the air; the god-like view of the ground below and the thud of the tyres as they landed safely back on the ground set her pulse racing. She emerged into the gusty, mid-February wind with a grin on her face like a cat that had got the cream. Maybe this quest would involve some more long-distance air travel. If so, bring it on!

Her destination was a historic tower in Iqbal Park, a huge open space in the centre of Lahore. A taxi from the airport drove her to the gates and she set off on foot for the monument that she could see in the distance. All would have been well if the kite-flying festival had not been taking place in the park at the same time! Asha stopped and gazed in wonder at the brightly coloured array of kites swooping and diving around in the sky above her. They came in all shapes and sizes – regular diamond-shaped kites with long fluttering tails made of sparkly materials; high-flying box kites that looked too big and heavy even to get off the ground; hexagonal Bermuda kites with their kaleidoscope of dazzling colours and six-sided Japanese kites that flew as easily as birds. There were even inflatable kites and – the ones Asha liked best – pairs of fighting kites. The girl forgot all about her mission and sat on a bench, gazing with excitement and wonder at the aerial dance of the fighting kites that sparred with each other like graceful, flying boxers.

Asha had seen kite displays before. They were popular in her home state of West Bengal. But she had never been so close to one or felt a part of it before. Now she did. So, without a further thought, she hurried over to the striped booth tent where kites could be hired to join in the fun. At least, that was the intention. It did not prove to be quite as easy as it looked. Asha chose a stunt kite, a large delta-shaped kite controlled by two strings that appealed to her because it had a dragon's face on it. It was actually quite a scary face with huge bulging eyes and sharp teeth that looked like it was about to bite you. But it proved impossible to get into the air! Like any other skill, kite-flying needs a certain amount of practice and cannot be done straight away. Luckily, an elderly couple took pity on Asha and showed her what she was doing wrong. Soon, the glaring dragon was airborne and before long, it was swooping around in the sky along with all the other kites. Asha felt elated!

The sun was starting to go down before the youngster came to her senses. She had lost all track of time and of her reason for being in Pakistan. Returning the kite to the hiring booth, Asha ran across the wide park in the gathering darkness until she reached the monument. She read the plaque explaining how the lighthouse-like tower was put up to commemorate the moment, back in 1940, when the people of Pakistan decided they wanted the creation of a new independent country, which was awarded seven years later. She was wondering what to do next when her right hand began to twitch in a now familiar fashion. Scrabbling for her diary, she just had time to jot down the next set of coordinates before the tigers ceased communicating with her again ...

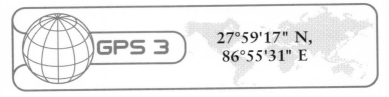

GPS 3   27°59'17" N, 86°55'31" E

'All's well that ends well,' she said to herself, feeling pleased she had completed this second stage of her mission.

It was almost dark and too late to get back to the airport to catch a flight out of Lahore. So she checked into a small, family-run hotel opposite the gates of the park. For supper, Asha chose a meat khari and rice, the speciality dish of Pakistan served in a piping hot metal bowl mounted on a wooden plate. Then she turned in for the night, determined to get on with her mission from now on and let nothing delay or stop her.

As Asha emerged from her hotel the following morning, Dhalia Menokki was waiting for her! Nazir Kapoor had sent his trusted supervisor to bring back the girl he imagined was his daughter. Having found Corinne missing, the factory owner had assumed she had run away to avoid the forced marriage to Narmal Vazkar. This was confirmed when Ranjana's father, his long-time friend and bank manager, came round to show him the photograph sent on his daughter's mobile. Dhalia Menokki was duly dispatched to Agra to catch her, but the fugitive had moved on. But where? That was the question! It was quickly answered as the bank manager gave Nazir Kapoor complete access to Corinne's private account. The string of credit card transactions laid a clear trail that could easily be followed. By wasting so much time yesterday and being forced to stay overnight, Asha had given her pursuers time to catch up with her. Worse still, having never used a credit card before and not really understanding how it worked, Asha had no idea she was giving away her exact position every time she used it!

Asha and the tough, unfriendly woman caught sight of each other at the same instant.

'Hello, Corinne,' called Dhalia Menokki, with exaggerated politeness. 'I've come to take you home.'

Asha did not reply. She just took to her heels and raced across the busy road, dodging the furiously hooting cars and buses. She headed into the park, hoping her youth and fitness would allow her to put some distance between herself and her pursuer. But Dhalia Menokki was a formidable foe. She could run like the wind and seemed to have endless stamina. When Asha grew tired and started to slow down, her enemy pressed on relentlessly and caught her up with every stride. Soon, the girl felt Dhalia Menokki's hand reaching out to grab her shoulder and realised she would soon be caught. Adrenalin surging through her body, Asha conjured up a sudden increase of speed and swerved down a side path, gaining a few valuable seconds in which to dodge behind a nearby red-and-white-striped tent. It was the kite-hiring booth! Crouching near the ground, Asha looked up to find the owner glaring down at her with a puzzled frown. Then, she had an idea!

Jumping up, she thrust some money into the man's hand and pointed to the same stunt kite she had rented yesterday. Using her newly learned skills, she soon got her mighty dragon airborne and was waiting for Dhalia Menokki as the woman came striding purposely towards her over the grass. Then, Asha swung into action. Carefully pulling the dual strings, she brought the kite swooping down over her enemy's head, forcing Dhalia Menokki to duck

and dive as if avoiding attack by a giant bird.
Purposefully, Asha went for the kill. Dropping the
dragon in an arc of breathtaking speed, Asha
whacked her supervisor around the head with the
kite like a boxer delivering a knockout blow.
Thwarted, Dhalia Menokki gave a muffled groan
and collapsed to the ground like a sack of potatoes.
Asha was free to escape!

Throwing down the kite and leaving her enemy
unconscious on the ground, Asha fled from Iqbal
Park and caught a taxi to the airport. By the time
Dhalia Menokki reached the departure lounge, her
throbbing head carefully bandaged, her quarry was
already high above the clouds, heading towards the
snowy mountains of Nepal.

Chapter 5

Goddess of the Sky

As the plane began its descent towards Kathmandu, the largest city in Nepal, Asha found her eyes drawn to the man sitting next to her. It was hard to tell his age because his face was hidden by a long grey beard and he wore lots of necklaces and beads over his flowing white robes. He was obviously some kind of guru or holy man and Asha felt very in awe of him, pretending to read the flight magazine whilst peeking at him curiously over the pages. But the guru had noticed Asha's furtive glances and decided to engage with her in conversation.

'Please tell me,' he said, in a gentle voice. 'What is a young lady like yourself doing travelling to Nepal on her own?'

'Sightseeing,' replied Asha shyly, deciding to say as little as possible.

'Ah, I see,' replied the guru, softly. 'And what,

pray, are you hoping to see?'

'I don't know yet,' said Asha, not daring to reveal her true destination in case he was going there too and wanted to accompany her.

There was a short pause. Then, pulling thoughtfully on the ends of his straggly beard, the man said, 'Something tells me you are deeply troubled. You have the look of someone with the weight of the world on their young shoulders.'

Asha said nothing. She just sat, looking out of the window and wished the plane would land soon.

'Your silence is telling me I am correct,' continued her companion. 'Most certainly, you are not a sightseer. Perhaps you are a criminal on the run?'

'I most certainly am not, sir!' retorted Asha, indignantly.

She expected the guru to question her further, but instead he just sat rocking backwards and forwards, chanting quietly to himself. When he had finished, he turned to Asha and smiled.

'I was praying for you then,' he explained. 'Praying that you will find peace.'

'Thank you, sir,' said Asha, politely. 'But I will only find peace when I have completed what I have to do.'

'Ah, I see!' said the guru, nodding his head. 'You have something important to accomplish. Then let me tell you a little story ...

'Once, there was a lion, a monkey and a mouse. They stood together on the edge of a fast-flowing river. On the other side was a beautiful orchard full of lush grass, shady trees and abundant food. All three animals wanted to live there. But they had to cross the river first.

"I'm not scared of a little water!" roared the lion. "I'm the King of Beasts, so nothing can prevent me from getting what I want."

'With that, he plunged into the river. But the water was icy cold and took his breath away. The lion found he could not swim properly in the frigid water, and was swept away by the current. So, up stepped the monkey.

"I'm clever," he chuckled. "I'm going to use my cunning brain to get what I want."

'So, the monkey grabbed hold of a creeper vine and tried to swing across the river to the other side. But the creeper broke! The monkey fell into the icy water and was swept away like the lion. That just left the mouse.

"I am very little," said the mouse, "and the river is very wide. But I can do this if I try. Nobody is going to help me. I must rely on myself if I'm going to get what I want."

'With that, the brave little mouse jumped from log to log across the freezing water and the swirling current. He was often tempted to give up, but he kept on thinking he could do it and, at last, he reached the other side. Now the mouse has everything he wants and is at peace, thanks to his courage and self-belief.'

'That was a lovely story,' said Asha with a smile. 'I will always remember it – especially when my own river seems impossible to cross.'

After that, not a word was exchanged between the two travellers for the rest of the flight.

Changing planes at Kathmandu airport, Asha made the short half-an-hour flight to Lukla in a small blue-and-white passenger aircraft with propellers on both wings.

The village, at around 2,000 feet, was the gateway to the Himalayas and every tourist, approaching the mountains from Nepal, had to pass through it. Asha was advised to remain in the village for at least a day to get used to the altitude, but she was impatient to complete this leg of her quest and moved on straight away. She travelled by helicopter to Namche Bazaar, a village at 3,440 metres that relied on income almost entirely from visiting tourists. Here, the air was much thinner and, at first, Asha had difficulty in catching her breath.

'Hope I don't have to run anywhere fast,' she thought.

Having checked into a comfortable-looking lodge, Asha wandered around the streets in search of some supper. She wanted to try some authentic Nepalese cuisine, but all the establishments catered for tourists and served Western food. She ended up in a German restaurant eating Italian pizza served with garlic French bread. She found it all delicious! Asha turned in around mid-evening, ready for a very early start the next day. She had been told that spectacular views of the world's highest mountain could be had from the HQ building in Sagarmatha National Park, just above the village. So that's where she was heading at daybreak.

It was a long trek up the steep slope to the big wooden building, but Asha was fresh and fighting fit. At first, she thought her long climb would be in vain because a thick veil of misty cloud obscured all the views from the park. But the morning sun soon burned this away and Asha was treated to the spectacular sight of the huge mountain towering over everything in the distance. It looked breathtakingly beautiful, a patchwork of grey rock and pure white snow set against a backdrop of the clearest blue sky. In Kolkata, the sky was often yellowy grey due to the smog and pollution from the city. Here, away from civilisation, it was a shimmering, crystal blue that made Asha want to cry. She understood now how this place got its name. Sagarmatha is the modern Nepalese name for the mountain, meaning 'goddess of the sky.'

Asha took a photo of the beautiful view on her mobile. She was so engrossed in the moment that she felt quite annoyed when the tigers contacted her with the coordinates of her next destination:

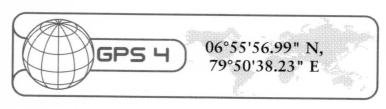

GPS 4   06°55'56.99" N, 79°50'38.23" E

'I want to stay here longer!' she shouted out loud. 'This place makes me feel ...'

That was as far as she got. A rough hand clamped itself over her mouth and she felt her arm

being twisted up painfully behind her back.
Struggling fiercely as she was bundled towards a
nearby helicopter, she managed to catch a glimpse
of her assailant out of the corner of her eye and saw
the cruel face of Dhalia Menokki smirking back
at her.

'You've led me a merry dance, Miss Kapoor,' she
snarled. 'But not for much longer!'

There was an animal cage in the back of the
helicopter and Asha realised she was going to be
put into it!

Asha realised that her captor would have to let
go of her with one hand in order to open the door.
Which hand would it be? Asha calculated that it
would be the one covering her mouth. So, the
moment this hand started to move, Asha bit it as
hard as she possibly could. Dhalia Menokki let out
an ear-piercing scream and loosened her vice-like
grip. That was all Asha needed. She was off,
sprinting like a gazelle across open grassland
towards a heavily wooded forest area.

It took little more than a few strides for Asha to realise she was not going to be able to keep this pace up for long. The air was too thin! She could hardly breathe. What was worse, Dhalia Menokki had wisely decided not to pursue her on foot this time. Asha's assailant was coming after her in the helicopter, hovering low over the grass and gaining on her with every passing second. Her lungs bursting and her legs feeling like lead, Asha slowed down and was helpless to prevent Dhalia Menokki from landing the helicopter, grabbing her long hair and dragging her roughly to the ground.

'Got you this time, my beauty!' shrieked Dhalia, triumphantly, as she threw Asha into the cage in the back of the helicopter.

The cage was designed for a dog, so there was barely room for Asha inside. Even so, she was squashed in and the door slammed and locked shut behind her. In a moment of wild panic, Asha thought of revealing her true identity, but realised it was a mad idea and opted to wait and see what would happen next.

Meanwhile, Dhalia Menokki tried to ring Nazir Kapoor on her mobile to say 'mission accomplished,' but with no signal due to the mountains, she was forced to fly to some open, stony ground before she could make the phone call. As Dhalia got out of the helicopter and stood below a high outcrop of rock, pressing the numbers for Kolkata on her phone, a Bengal tiger appeared right above her. In an instant, the creature made a menacing faff-faffing sound, indicating that it was about to attack. The tiger then launched itself over the edge of the cliff, sliding down the slope amidst an ever-increasing number of rocks.

The avalanche hit Dhalia like an express train and almost buried her. It rolled on, the huge tiger mixed up in the middle of it, and hit the helicopter, turning it over on its side. Following the impact, the door flew open, but the cage remained locked and Asha could not get out. Then she saw the tiger, panting and bleeding, as it struggled to free itself from the rubble and limped over to her. With one deft slash of its mighty paw, the animal tore open the cage door before collapsing onto the rocks beside the helicopter.

'Go!' said the injured tiger, talking directly into Asha's mind. 'I have travelled from my homeland and sacrificed myself to free you. Go and continue your mission. Now!'

Despite her ordeal and the painfully thin air, Asha ran all the way back to the HQ building and then down the steep trail to the village, tears rolling down her cheeks every single step of the way.

Chapter 6

Waves of Emotion

Asha's love affair with international air travel began to wane when she was delayed for six hours at Kathmandu airport en route for Sri Lanka.

'Please may I know what the problem is?' she asked the friendly-looking man at the information desk.

'Certainly, madam,' he replied with a smile. 'There has been some kind of volcanic disturbance under the Indian Ocean between the Seychelles and the Maldives. This has been accompanied by strong winds and heavy rain that have delayed the arrival of our incoming aircraft. Barring any further problems, your flight to Colombo will depart at the revised time of 0600 hours.'

So Asha had no choice but to spend the night on a modern and very uncomfortable sofa, trying to sleep despite all the bustle going on around her and the constant BING-BONG of the airport announcements.

This delay felt particularly exasperating because, up until now, Asha had prided herself on completing each stage of her mission quickly, apart from the blip with the kite flying. She had worked out, from her original briefing by the tigers, that seven quests in a single year meant each one needed to last about six to seven weeks. If anyone took any longer than that, the amount of time left for the following quests would be cut down and this could make all the difference between eventual success and failure. So far, Asha had taken about ten days to complete the first three parts of her challenge. So she was well on schedule, but she still did not know her remaining seven destinations and how long it would take to reach them.

Eventually, at 5 am, the flight to Sri Lanka was called. Asha and the other bleary-eyed passengers rose from their chairs like zombies and lined up, aching and silent, in the departure lounge. Asha was also disappointed that she was leaving Nepal without sampling any proper Nepalese cuisine, so she cheered up when the flight attendants served some dal bhat for breakfast. This is the national dish of Nepal, eaten twice a day, consisting of a tasty mixture of rice and spiced lentils. Served with a flatbread called a roti, it tasted lovely and settled the teenager's stomach for the long flight south over India. There was no sign of the storms that were troubling other parts of the region and the plane landed on time around mid-afternoon. Having only a rucksack on her back, she did not have to endure the long wait for luggage to appear and so hurried out of Colombo airport, keen to complete this stage of her quest, take in some quick sights of Sri Lanka and get out again on the same day.

She did not have far to travel this time. Hailing a taxi, she made her way to the fort area right in the heart of the city. Her destination was the tallest building in the capital and the second tallest in the whole of south Asia.

Asha did not realise, however, that it had two towers.

'I thought that there were only twin towers in New York,' she remarked to the taxi driver, a round-faced man with a little moustache who kept eating boiled sweets.

'No, they were destroyed in the terrible events of 9/11,' he replied, noisily shifting a fruit bonbon from one side of his mouth to the other. 'Our skyscrapers have the same design that the twin towers in America had.'

Unfortunately, Asha was not in a position to take in any of this information. She was too busy writing down the coordinates of her next port of call as dictated to her by the tigers ...

GPS 5   06°06'05.10" S, 105°25'21.50" E

Returning to the airport in the taxi, her business done, Asha was horrified to learn that the flight she wanted to take to Indonesia had been cancelled due to a strike by baggage-handlers in Java.

'How long before the dispute is settled?' she asked at the information desk.

The woman here was neither friendly nor helpful. She had been asked the same question fifty times already and had no answer to give.

'We don't know anything, madam,' she snapped. 'Keep your eye on the departure boards and listen for announcements.'

'Could I catch another flight?' suggested Asha, hopefully.

'All the flights to Java are cancelled,' sighed the woman, wearily. 'My advice to you, young lady, is to go sightseeing on our beautiful island and come back in 48 hours to find out what's going on.'

Unable to proceed any further for two days, Asha felt so frustrated that she thought she would burst. Then she remembered what her father used to tell her about accepting things as they are rather than always wishing that they were different.

'I can't do anything about this situation,' she said to herself. 'So I should use this time to relax, recharge my batteries ready for when I am able to continue.'

Once this idea had taken a hold, Asha felt all her anxiety and frustration draining away and a sense of excitement rising up within her. She was free for a while. She could take the rest that she needed.

Looking at a tourist map she bought from a vending machine, there were a number of places she would have liked to have visited, but they were all too far away. So she decided on Negombo, a holiday resort just a few kilometres up the coast from the capital. The bus journey only took half an hour, meaning that Asha arrived in time to check in to one of the many hotels on the seafront and wander down onto the beach to watch the sunset. It was so beautiful – a dazzling mixture of bright orange and luminous pink that made Asha feel like she was dreaming. She had only ever been to the seaside once before and, on that day, it had rained. Now here she was on a tropical island, standing with her toes in the crystal clear water and the warm wind ruffling her hair, with nothing to do and nothing to worry about for the next two days. She held her arms out wide.

'Thank you,' she said out loud. 'It is indeed an honour to have been chosen for this quest.'

'Who are you talking to?' asked a friendly voice behind her.

Spinning round, Asha found herself looking at a boy, about her own age, with a tanned body and beautiful white teeth that seemed to flash when he smiled.

'I was just talking to myself,' answered Asha, feeling foolish and annoyed at being overheard.

'And what's this quest you're on?' continued the boy, curiously.

'I didn't say anything about a quest,' lied Asha.

'Yes, you did,' he replied. 'I heard you!'

'No, I didn't,' insisted Asha.

'Yes, you did!' repeated the boy.

'I didn't! I didn't! I didn't!' shrieked Asha, furiously. 'I never mentioned the word "quest"! Is that clear?'

'Yeah, sure!' exclaimed the stranger, backing away. 'Sorry. I didn't mean to upset you.'

Fighting back some tears, Asha turned on her heel and ran back up the white sandy beach to the hotel.

She met the boy again the next morning. After a supper of fiery, coconut-flavoured curry, a good night's sleep and a compote of pineapple, mango and passion fruit for breakfast, she felt in much better shape and went over to apologise for her behaviour the previous evening. She was readily forgiven and the two teenagers strolled down the beach to watch the local fishermen launching their boats in search of lobsters and prawns. The boy told Asha that his name was Rob and that he came from Edinburgh in Scotland. His parents, both teachers, had given up their stressful jobs and escaped to this popular resort where they ran a bar. Rob was old enough to have finished school, so he spent his days water skiing and windsurfing like a millionaire playboy.

'Are you lonely?' he asked, suddenly.

'What a strange thing to say,' replied Asha. 'Why do you ask?'

'Because I get lonely, living here so far away from my friends,' he admitted. 'And you have the same sort of look about you.'

'So what are you suggesting?' wondered Asha.

'Let's be friends,' chuckled Rob. 'Then we can be lonely together!'

Asha warmed to this idea. Her work and family commitments meant she had never had a proper friend before – much less a male one. Rajat, who carried supplies around the factory in Kolkata, used to chat to her sometimes when Dhalia Menokki was not looking, but he was older than her and hardly a friend. Now she found herself in the company of someone her own age who seemed kind and genuine. So, she thought to herself as Rob suggested a sharbat (a delicious Sri Lankan drink made from crushed fruit or flower petals) at one of the beach cafes, why not? You're in the middle of a once-in-a-lifetime experience. What have you got to lose by sharing it with a friend?

Rob and Asha spent an idyllic couple of days together in Negombo. They swam, they chatted, they laughed together. As the time to leave drew near, Asha felt she had known Rob all her life and hated the thought of being parted from him. But go she must. So she felt compelled to give him a decent reason … and that meant telling him the truth. Ignoring the tigers' insistence on absolute secrecy, she sat on a rock looking out to sea and gently tapped the boy's suntanned shoulder.

'You know that question you asked me when we first met?' she began.

'About the quest?' said Rob.

'That's right,' agreed Asha. 'Well, I'm about to

tell you something very, very important. It's so
important that …'

She did not get any further as the tsunami
warning sirens sounded all along the beach.

An undersea eruption in the Indian Ocean had
caused a gigantic wave that was sweeping towards
the western shores of Sri Lanka. Asha and Rob
could see it coming – a moving wall of water
rushing towards the shore that grew ever higher as
it approached – and they joined the crowds of
screaming holidaymakers fleeing inland to safety.
In the noise and confusion, Asha became separated
from Rob and, hearing the huge wave crashing
down behind her, she had to fend for herself by
clambering up the fire escape outside one of the
hotel buildings and taking refuge on the roof.
From this safe vantage point, she saw the water
swirling into the buildings below and caught sight
of several figures scrambling up telegraph poles
like monkeys to get clear of it. One of these figures
looked very familiar. It was Rob. He was safe!

Thanks to the early warning system, no one was killed by the tsunami. Asha felt a surge of relief rush through her, followed by a steely resolve to leave the resort and continue with her mission. She had been prevented from revealing her secret at the last moment and had nearly lost her life. It was time to count her blessings and move on. So, without saying goodbye to Rob, she waded through the fast-receding waters until she reached dry ground. Once safely inland, she caught a taxi to the frantic airport where she found flights to Indonesia had resumed. As hundreds wanted to leave the island due to the tsunami, Asha had to queue for hours. Using Corinne's credit card, once again, to buy a ticket to Java, she left on the last flight of the day. Her head was totally focused on the task in front of her, but her heart still lingered on the beautiful beach where she had met her first true friend.

Chapter 7

Scream, Scream, Scream!

Dhalia Menokki was right behind Asha. Snarling with rage – the tigers were nowhere to be seen – the woman grabbed Asha and spun her around, recognising her immediately as an imposter …

'YOU!' shrieked Dhalia Menokki, furiously …

Asha woke up with a scream, sinking back onto her pillow with waves of relief flooding through her sweat-drenched body as she realised that it was only a vivid nightmare.

The youngster had arrived in Jakarta, the capital of Java, late the previous evening and had to spend the night in a ridiculously expensive hotel near the city's main airport. Her delight in flying had now completely evaporated following a two-hour delay in the skies above the island, circling round and round in a stack of airliners, each waiting its turn to land. She was now a hardened international traveller and aircraft, with all their associated problems and frustrations, were just a means to an end.

Turning over in the luxurious bed and throwing off the sweltering duvet, her thoughts returned to the matter of Dhalia Menokki. She imagined the woman was dead and that made her feel guilty. Asha did not ever want to feel responsible for anyone else's death. On the other hand, her old supervisor was unkind to the point of cruelty and was on a mission to capture a young woman and return her to a life of domestic drudgery. At least, Asha reasoned, she was no longer being pursued and was free to get on with her vital quest without further interference.

Had Asha been in the lobby of the hotel rather than in one of the bedrooms, she would have needed to make a drastic amendment to this last thought. Not having heard from Dhalia Menokki for a while, Nazir Kapoor had dispatched his friend and business partner Narmal Vazkar to find his runaway daughter instead. Narmal Vazkar needed no second bidding. He was deeply disappointed that his beautiful teenage bride had eluded him and was just as keen to get her back as her father. So, following the trail of credit card transactions, emailed to him via mobile phone from India, he had tracked his quarry down to this hotel and was sitting waiting for her to appear. Having only ever seen photographs of Corinne and never met her in the flesh, he had no idea the girl he was after was someone else. She had a pretty face and a trim little figure – and she was the girl he intended to marry!

At around 8 am, his target appeared and he followed her to the dining room, sitting a few tables away and watching her closely from behind a newspaper. Asha caused something of a disturbance by ordering chicken satay for breakfast. She was keen to keep sampling national dishes while she had the chance and these delicious mouthfuls of meat, mounted on bamboo skewers and dipped in a spicy peanut sauce, were the speciality dish of Java.

The hotel, however, was used to serving this dish for lunch or dinner, so it took a while for the chefs to satisfy Asha's order. This gave ample time for Narmal Vazkar to study his prey and weigh up his options. He decided to follow the girl while she carried out whatever she had come to Indonesia to do and then strike when the right moment presented itself.

Feeling slightly queasy after her highly spiced breakfast, Asha checked out and took a taxi to Jakarta's second airport from which flights could be chartered. To her great delight, she found there was a tourist flight scheduled to leave in forty minutes for the volcanic island that was her next destination. It was a helicopter flight in a large ex-military machine capable of seating six people. Four of the seats were already booked. Asha bought the fifth and a rather large, balding middle-aged man (Narmal Vazkar) standing right behind her snapped up the last one with a whoop of joy.

Asha sensed the man staring at her as the big

chopper swung out to sea in a graceful arc and clattered towards the Sunda Strait, between Java and Sumatra. Narmal kept looking at Asha in a way that he did not do to the other four passengers. He soon noticed her looking back and, anxious not to arouse any suspicions, gave a quick smile and spoke to Asha by way of a diversion.

'Did you know this volcano erupted in 1883, killing around 36,000 people?' he asked.

'I was just reading about that in my guide book,' replied Asha, trying to deter him from speaking to her further.

'They made a film about it years ago,' he continued. 'One of those dreadful disaster movies. The title was *East of Java*. How could they get it so wrong? It's west of Java, is it not?'

Asha nodded and smiled in agreement, returning to her book as quickly as she could. She read that the volcanic ash from the enormous eruption had spread all around the world, making the moon appear blue in some places and the sky blood red in others. The Norwegian painter, Edvard Munch, used this dazzling, flame-like sky in his famous picture, *The Scream*.

'If that fat, annoying man doesn't leave me alone,' thought Asha, angrily, 'that's exactly what I'm going to do – scream!'

As the huge, cone-shaped island came into view, Asha experienced a moment of panic as she wondered if the tigers expected her to set foot on it. If they did, this trip was a waste of time and she needed to get back to Jakarta and hire a boat instead. But all was well. Like the mountain in Nepal, it seemed enough that the girl had managed to reach the place and had seen it clearly. She soon felt the familiar tingling in her right hand and grabbed the diary from her rucksack in time to scribble down the next set of coordinates:

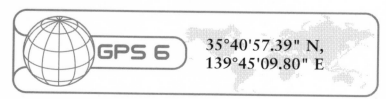

GPS 6

35°40'57.39" N,
139°45'09.80" E

'What are you doing?' asked an unwelcome voice.

Looking up, Asha found Narmal Vazkar leaning over her shoulder in a particularly close and uncomfortable way.

'Oh, nothing,' replied Asha, casually.

'Yes, you were,' continued the man with a little laugh. 'You just wrote something down.'

'Just a few notes,' said Asha, trying her hardest to dismiss him. But he was not to be deterred!

'They weren't notes,' insisted Narmal Vazkar. 'I just saw a jumble of numbers and letters. Was it a code?'

'That's right,' agreed Asha, hastily. 'I was writing in code.'

'How interesting!' exclaimed Narmal Vazkar, smiling and leaning across even further. 'Explain it to me!'

ARRGHHH! screamed Asha, inside.

Luckily, at that moment, the pilot made an urgent announcement over the intercom.

'Ladies and gentlemen,' he said. 'I'm afraid we shall have to cut short your pleasure flight this morning. We're receiving warnings of increasing seismic activity in the area and it's possible that an earthquake may occur somewhere along the chain of Indonesian islands. So we must return to base at once.'

Asha did not join in the big sigh of disappointment emitted by her fellow passengers. She had completed her business and was glad to be getting back as quickly as possible. But she did gaze out of the window for a last look at the famous volcano that she would probably never see again in her life. It loomed grey and menacing, with a wisp of smoke hanging over the nozzle-like hole at the top. It looked like a gigantic boil on the surface of Earth! Asha felt frightened of it. It was a truly awe-inspiring sight … but not a happy or uplifting one.

Narmal Vazkar made his move as soon as the helicopter landed back at the airport. While the pilot and other passengers were walking ahead, he grabbed Asha before she could scream and, gripping her arm very tightly, shoved her into a small workshop full of oil drums and tools.

'Who are you and what do you want?' shrieked Asha.

'I am Narmal Vazkar, your intended husband,' he said, curtly. 'What I want is to marry you instead of having to chase you halfway around the world.'

Asha's response was to spit angrily in the man's face. For a moment, he looked ready to hit her. Then he gave a sickly smile.

'You are a spirited one, Corinne Kapoor,' he whispered, menacingly. 'You have gone to such lengths to avoid marrying me. But I will break your spirit, my dear, do not worry about that. Women should always do what men tell them. The world is in a sorry mess because women do not know how to obey.'

'I've never heard such vile rubbish in my life …' began Asha, but her captor silenced her by thrusting his clenched fist under her chin.

'Silence!' he shouted. 'You have said enough both in word and in deed. From now on, you will say nothing unless I tell you to. Now come with me. We have to catch a flight to Bali. Tomorrow we will wed.'

Asha did as she was told and travelled the short distance to the neighbouring island without speaking a word. She longed to tell her fellow passengers on the short-haul airliner that she was being forced to travel against her will, but Narmal Vazkar watched her like a hawk and prevented her from leaving his side.

I'll bide my time and wait for a chance to escape, thought Asha, bravely.

It did not come! As soon as they reached Ngurah Rai, Bali's international airport, Asha found herself pushed into a taxi and driven down to Jimbaran, a beach resort on the coast. In normal circumstances, Asha would have loved this place. The sun was setting over the soft sandy beach, illuminating the rows of open air seafood cafes and restaurants selling freshly caught fish grilled over a flaming barbeque of coconut husks. It would have been just to her taste, but this evening she had no appetite or interest in food. She was frightened, very frightened, about what was going to happen to her tomorrow. More importantly, she was worried about not being able to continue her quest.

Asha spent all night locked in a garage beside a rented holiday villa at the end of a lonely track. She banged on the door and screamed for help until her throat was hoarse, but nobody came. Around midnight, Narmal Vazkar opened the door and thrust a plate of sandwiches and a drink at her.

'Sleep well, my lovely,' he called. 'It's your big day tomorrow!'

The hotel she was taken to the next morning was decked out with tropical flowers. It hosted weddings on the beach nearly every day and nobody noticed anything unusual about a middle-aged man taking a surly-looking bride to exchange vows in front of the ever-smiling officials.

Asha felt the first tremor under her feet as she stood listening to the opening words of the ceremony being read to her. She said nothing, not daring to believe her luck. The second tremor was a major one, quickly followed by a third that made the buildings shake to their very foundations. The warning had been correct. A major earthquake was striking Bali!

This was the chance that Asha had been waiting for! She lifted the bottom of her long wedding dress and raced up the beach, dodging the falling debris and screaming crowds. Narmal Vazkar was slower off the mark and it proved his undoing. As he started to race after his fleeing bride, a lifeguard tower toppled over on its side and crashed down, trapping him under a heavy pile of twisted metal. Now it was his turn to scream – but not for long. His cries were soon silenced as a further tremor brought an enormous palm tree crashing down on top of him as well.

The earthquake put the Ngurah Rai airport out of action for a couple of days, but Asha was happy to rest after her terrible ordeal. She hid out at a rented villa and then flew on to Japan the moment the island's airport was operational again.

Chapter 8

Emperors and Kings

Sitting on the plane as it descended smoothly towards Tokyo International Airport, Asha wondered how the real Corinne Kapoor was getting on. Had she married her beloved Devesh yet? Were they living somewhere in secret, madly in love and blissfully happy? She hoped so!

Asha felt eternally grateful to her 'double' for financing her expensive quest. There were still four places to visit after this, so she prayed that Corinne's credit card would continue to hold out. She had no idea that, at this very minute, the latest transactions were being closely studied and plans drawn up to end the chase once and for all.

Asha fell in love with Tokyo the moment she entered the city. The bustling crowds made it feel like home, but this place was modern, and clean, and had bright lights everywhere you looked. Asha had never seen such vivid colours! It was mid-evening and the multitude of neon signs glowed and flashed in the darkness like a giant firework display that never stopped. Asha got out of her taxi before reaching her destination and wandered about, gazing up in awe at the electronic light-show above her head. That's when she (literally) bumped into a boy called Al.

Al was a short, bespectacled fifteen-year-old from Omaha in the United States. He had untidy hair, several spots and a nervous tick that made him keep pushing his glasses back up his nose … but he had a friendly smile and Asha felt the need for some companionship just at this moment.

'I'm sorry, did I hurt you …?' she asked, anxiously.

'Nah,' replied Al, casually. 'Just a few bruises and a dislocated shoulder, but otherwise I'm okay. Fancy some sushi?'

Asha had already thought about sampling Japan's famous national dish, so she readily accepted.

'Tell you what,' added Al, 'let's go to one of those outfits where you choose your supper swimmin' around. You should choose a flat fish, so I can say: What's a plaice like this doing in a girl like you? HA, HA, HA!'

Al was visiting Tokyo with his mother who was a buyer for an American electrical firm. She spent all of her time looking at the latest electronic gismos and gadgets, leaving him to his own devices. So Al was glad of some company, too.

'So what are you here for, Corinne?' he asked, over their bowls of tasty raw fish. 'Don't tell me. Let me guess. You're a top secret special agent, employed by a mysterious superpower, fighting single-handedly to save the world from destruction.'

'How did you guess?' she replied, barely able to contain herself from telling him that he was almost exactly right. 'And you?'

'Me?' he replied. 'I'm the King of Siam, here to visit the emperor.'

Mention of the emperor reminded Asha of her

mission to save the world.

'I must go,' she said, getting up hastily.

'Don't you like your sushi or something?' cried Al.

'It's lovely, but I have to be somewhere,' she explained.

'Okay,' he chuckled, jumping up too. 'I've got some yen to pay the bill ... and another yen to come with you! HA, HA, HA!'

Her destination was the home of the Japanese emperor. It was a beautiful building set in enormous grounds right in the heart of Tokyo. As Al and Asha walked towards it through the late-evening crowds, Al informed her that someone had once valued the three-and-a-half square kilometre site as being worth more than all the houses in California put together.

'I'm full of fascinating facts like that,' said Al. 'Wanna hear some more?'

'No, thanks,' replied Asha, firmly. 'Now if you don't mind leaving me alone, I have some important business to attend to.'

'Like what?' he demanded.

'Mind your own business,' she retorted, touching her nose.

'Please yourself,' sighed Al, walking away. 'But if you want to go to the toilet, you don't need to be so secretive about it!'

Asha hurried off on her own, Corinne's jewel-encrusted pen and leather-bound diary at the ready. But nothing happened! The tigers did not seem to recognise that she had reached her sixth milestone successfully and didn't send the coordinates of her next destination.

'What's wrong?' she wondered, a terrible sense of panic rising in her throat.

Then she realised the main building lay in darkness and she could not see it properly.

'I'll have to come back tomorrow,' she murmured, 'when it's light.'

Asha spent the night in a strange hotel full of tiny rooms with just enough space for one person. The sleeping space was an enclosed tube, rather like a coffin or a drawer in a mortuary, that slid in and out. Asha hated it, but she was so tired that she fell asleep straight away, despite her claustrophobic surroundings. She woke early, feeling refreshed, and after paying the very modest bill she hurried back to where she had been last night.

This time, there was no problem with communication from the tigers. She stood in the East Gardens – the only part of the complex open to visitors – and gazed across to the main building in the distance.

'I can see it clearly now, guys!' she called.

Immediately, her twitching hand felt compelled to write down the following coordinates:

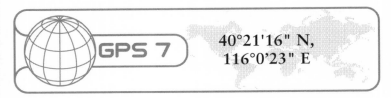

GPS 7

40°21'16" N,
116°0'23" E

With her business in Japan now concluded, Asha was keen to be on her way as swiftly as possible.

But, Asha's plans were thwarted when she found Al waiting for her at the entrance to the gardens.

'What happened to you last night?' he asked.

'I went to a hotel,' answered Asha.

'You might have told me,' complained Al, half-jokingly and half-annoyed. 'I waited for ages in the cold and dark.'

'Sorry,' said Asha.

'So did you get your business done?' Al asked.

'Yes, thanks,' she replied.

'Okay, O Mysterious One,' called Al, brightly. 'What are we doing today?'

'I don't know what you're doing, Al,' said Asha, 'but I'm leaving.'

His face fell!

'B-B-But you can't!' he cried. 'You've only just got here.'

Asha just shook her head.

'This means we're not going to spend a wildly exciting day together,' he sighed, pacing about wringing his hands together in a dramatic fashion.

'And you won't meet my mother who'll be blown away by you. You won't come and visit me in Omaha and wow all my nerdy friends as well. Nor will you suddenly realise how much you love me and marry me and have lots of babies who all grow up to be rich and successful and leave home so that we can grow old together with silvery grey hair and piles.'

Asha smiled and shook her head again.

'That's cool!' he exclaimed, cheerfully. 'I'd really hate that to happen. It's so corny!'

With that, he went on his way, calling goodbye and waving. Asha watched, laughing out loud, until he disappeared amidst the early-morning crowds hurrying to their places of work. Then Asha's usual determined frown returned to her face and she made her way to nearby Tokyo station, ready to tackle the next instalment of the all-important life-or-death quest.

Chapter 9

Triple Jeopardy

The city of Beijing, capital of The People's Republic of China, lay buried in a thick yellow haze.

Asha imagined this was the smog for which the place was infamous, a choking mixture of traffic fumes and smoke from thousands of coal-burning factory chimneys that made Beijing one of the most polluted cities in the world. Today, however, it was even worse. The sprawling metropolis, home to nearly 18 million people, was also in the grip of one of the dust storms that often blew in from the north, the result of wind erosion in the desert. This reduced visibility to only a few metres, making it very difficult to get around. Asha hoped that nobody would ask what she was doing in China and make her reply with 'sightseer'. On a day like this, there was nothing to be seen!

Unable to breathe properly and feeling the cold –

this was, after all, a Chinese winter with temperatures hovering around freezing – Asha hurried to a shop selling cheap military-style clothing and bought herself a warm jacket, a cap with a peak and a thick woollen scarf. She wound the latter around her neck and face, providing a mask for her mouth that prevented the worst of the dust from going down her throat. Muffled up like an Egyptian mummy, she made her way from the small and scrupulously clean hotel, where she had spent the night, to a coach station with billboards advertising excursions to the place she needed to visit next. Asha had been told that the smog cleared once you got away from the capital. She very much hoped so. It would be terrible to reach her destination and not receive contact from the tigers because she could not see anything!

*   *   *   *   *   *   *   *   *   *   *

Nazir Kapoor did not need details of Asha's latest

credit card transaction to find out where she was going. He had followed her in person from the hotel, almost losing her several times in the billowing dust, and had watched with his own eyes as she bought her ticket and queued up with the line of other visitors waiting to board the ultra-modern tour bus. The factory owner had a motto which he often quoted to his hard-pressed employees: If you want something done, do it yourself!

Now Nazir Kapoor was living up to his motto. He had given up on Dhalia Menokki and Narmal Vazkar and had travelled to China to capture his runaway daughter himself.

*   *   *   *   *   *   *   *   *   *   *

The Badaling Expressway was a new road that ran the 80-or-so kilometres from Beijing to Badaling, one of the places where China's most famous monument could best be seen and walked along. The tour bus made good time along the motorway, turning off and pulling into the vast car park that had been built to accommodate the millions of visitors that throng to the place every year. Nazir Kapoor was already there, having overtaken the coach in his powerful hire car. He stood squinting at the endless line of passengers getting off the bus. The air here was crystal clear and he had no trouble spotting the slight figure of his daughter – or so he thought! Asha's new outfit almost completely disguised her features and Nazir Kapoor would have needed to get up really close, or maybe even hear the girl's voice, before he realised she was not the true Corinne.

Climbing the steep steps to the top of the ramparts made Asha puff, but the view from the top took her breath away even more. The huge monument twisted away in both directions as far as the eye could see, following the up-and-down contours of the surrounding hills like a gigantic snake. Asha read in her guide book that its total length was 6,700 kilometres, that it took over a hundred years to build and was once manned by a million soldiers – not to mention the estimated two-to-three million Chinese workers believed to have lost their lives actually constructing it. These statistics, combined with the awe-inspiring views of the surrounding countryside, made Asha feel very small and she was glad when the tigers made contact once more, giving her the coordinates for the eighth destination:

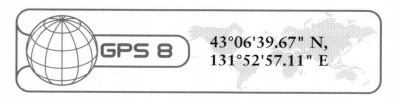

GPS 8

43°06'39.67" N,
131°52'57.11" E

As usual, Asha wanted to be on her way the moment her mission was accomplished, but today she was at the mercy of the tour bus which was not scheduled to depart for another couple of hours. The winter sun had now come out and was shining brightly, bathing everything in a rich, golden light. So, Asha decided to enjoy the sunshine by strolling along the ramparts with the lines of other visitors, who jabbered excitedly to each other and took lots of flash photographs with the latest digital cameras. None of these cameras, however, seemed to flash as brightly as the ring Corinne had given Asha when they exchanged identities. It appeared to have come alive, emitting several eye-piercing bursts of light as it caught the best of the afternoon sun.

Nazir Kapoor was waiting for his daughter at the bottom of a steep incline where the mighty stone walkway was only a short distance from the ground below.

'Hello, Corinne, my dear,' he called. 'We've been looking everywhere for you!'

Asha's first instinct was to run, but there were too many people milling about on the path and she knew she would not get away. So, she stood still and said nothing, allowing Nazir Kapoor to approach her with open arms and a smile.

'How long is it since I've held my princess?' he gushed. 'Come and have a hug with your father.'

Once the man had his arms around her, however,

the mood changed completely.

'You'd better come quietly, you wretched girl,' he whispered threateningly in Asha's ear. 'Otherwise you'll travel home in a trunk with your arms and legs tied with rope and a gag in your mouth.'

How was Asha going to get away this time? It seemed impossible. But as Nazir Kapoor released her from his threatening hug, she noticed her ring again and a wild idea came into her head. Timing it so that the sun was just emerging from a small cloud, she held up her hand and turned it left and right so the ring could catch as many rays as possible. FLASH! FLASH! The sudden blaze of light dazzled Nazir Kapoor and momentarily blinded him. He staggered about a little and then fell backwards over the parapet, disappearing from view with a startled cry. Asha wanted to look over the edge to see what had happened to him, but she dared not waste time or draw attention to herself. So, she just hurried away from the scene as quickly as she could.

Forgetting the tour bus, Asha paid for a taxi to take her all the way back to Beijing. That night, she celebrated with a splendid meal consisting of the capital's speciality, Peking roast duck, served with its traditional accompaniment of pancakes, spring onions and a sweet noodle sauce. This was followed by a bowl of lychees and cream that tasted so delicious that Asha asked for more.

Sitting up in her hotel bed that night, Asha set the alarm for her departure early the next morning. She felt a glow of pride that she had seen off all three of her pursuers and was now free to conclude her important quest in peace.

* * * * * * * * * * *

Asha enjoyed her flight from Beijing to the far east coast of Russia. It was a small short-haul airliner packed with wealthy Chinese and Russian businessmen who were obviously making the most of the rapid economic rise of their respective countries. Asha sat in the back row, turning the ring round and round on her finger. It had brought her luck, just as Corinne predicted. By saving her from Nazir Kapoor, the ring had also saved her mission and that was the most important thing of all. Asha wondered who she should pass the ring onto next. She decided to keep it on her finger until she found someone who really needed good luck.

The moment she got off the plane, the under-dressed teenager began to shiver. She had abandoned her Chinese outfit in favour of a T-shirt and jeans, but these clothes were most unsuitable for visiting a region close to the Arctic Circle in the middle of winter. Jumping into a taxi at the airport, she made straight for an outdoor clothing store and kitted herself out in warm boots, a thick coat and a Russian hat with earflaps. She was very careful to avoid buying any real fur. The sad plight of the tigers was never far from her mind and the idea of wearing clothes made from helpless animals made her feel sick.

The city in which Asha found herself was much bigger than she expected. It was a huge port with a long history and a close association with the mighty Russian navy. Asha liked ships and very much regretted that her quest had not given her the chance to sail on one. Still, she resisted the temptation to go down to the busy harbour, to watch all the comings and goings, and made straight for her next destination in another taxi. It was not hard to find – a long, low building of enormous size with private cars, hire cars, buses, mini-buses, coaches, taxis and any other manner of transport pulling up in front of it to disgorge or collect passengers every minute of the day.

Fighting her way through the hustle and bustle, Asha stood squarely in front of the building and waited for contact from the tigers. It did not happen. At first, the girl was puzzled. According to her mobile phone, she was in exactly the right place and looking at her stated destination in broad daylight. Then she realised there must be another spot somewhere nearby that she would need to reach before this stage of her task was completed.

Buying a platform ticket from a machine, she wandered around the bustling terminus in search of some special landmark or feature. She found it on one of the mainline platforms, a small memorial tower with a plaque beneath it marking the end of the line for the Trans-Siberian Railway. The moment she finished reading the information, her right hand began to tremble once more and she involuntarily began writing down the coordinates of her next destination:

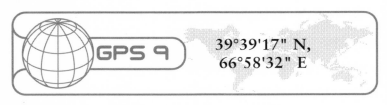

GPS 9

39°39'17" N, 66°58'32" E

Sitting on a nearby wooden bench, Asha took out her mobile and looked up the location of the coordinates. It was Samarkand, an ancient city right in the heart of Asia on the great Silk Road from China. What was the best way to get there? She could fly, but that meant all the bother of finding the airport and waiting for a flight. Alternatively, she could travel on one of the mighty trains which stood right beside her and departed every few hours. She decided to do the latter, hurrying to buy herself a special-offer open ticket (that permitted her to travel anywhere in Russia by train) and some magazines and sweets to pass the time on the journey. Asha calculated that it would take about seven days to travel down to Samarkand, changing trains at a place called Novosibirsk.

There was an empty carriage near the back of the train and Asha settled down in a seat by the window. As the long train began to rev its engines prior to departure, Dhalia Menokki came striding along the platform, glaring in at every window. Asha's blood ran cold as she hid herself behind the window curtain. So Dhalia was still alive – and out to catch her elusive prey, if the ferocious scowl on the woman's cruel face was anything to go by.

Worse was to follow. As the last-minute arrivals

were crowding into Asha's carriage, Narmal Vazkar came hurrying along outside the train, his right arm in a sling.

So he was not dead, either! Both her enemies boarded the train, clearly hunting for Asha. Feeling a rising sense of panic in her chest, Asha got up to leave the train, much to the surprise of her fellow passengers. But, as she reached up to the luggage rack for her bag, she glimpsed Nazir Kapoor hobbling along the platform. He scrambled on board just before the guard blew the final departure whistle. Asha could not believe her eyes! He must have survived his fall with only a sprained or broken ankle. Now all three of her adversaries were on the train, threatening to prevent the conclusion of her quest. What could she do? The answer was nothing! Next moment, the guard's whistle emitted a shrill PHEEP and the Trans-Siberian Express chuffed out of the station to begin its mighty journey across Mother Russia. Asha could not escape now. She was trapped!

All sorts of wild thoughts ran through Asha's mind. Could she jump off the train when it slowed for a bend? Could she pull the emergency cord and escape during the ensuing confusion? Could she call the security guard and claim she was being stalked? She soon realised none of these ideas would work and thought of the more prosaic idea of hiding in the toilet. That was ridiculous too because it was a crowded train and the toilet would be in use all the time. Then Asha remembered the luggage van between the carriages where large cases and other unwieldy goods were stored. Holding her breath that she would not be spotted by her adversaries, Asha left her seat and nervously walked along the swaying corridor to the luggage van. It was full of wooden crates and big cardboard boxes. When no one was looking, Asha rearranged the cargo to make herself a hidey-hole where she could sit and not be seen. She even made herself a seat and felt comfortable and safe, like an animal hiding away from danger in a cosy burrow. The difficulty was going to know when to get off the train at Novosibirsk – but that was still over two days away. CLICKEDY-CLACK, CLICKEDY-CLACK went the train, lulling Asha into a deep and much-needed sleep.

*   *   *   *   *   *   *   *   *   *   *

Samarkand proved to be as exotic and beautiful as its romantic name suggested. Marco Polo, one of the first Europeans to travel across Asia, described it as a 'very large and splendid city'. It was full of noisy markets and bazaars, all of which Asha longed to visit. But she turned down the temptation, focusing only on reaching the very oldest part of the city where her penultimate destination lay.

The journey had been totally uneventful. Asha's clever hiding place had served her well and she had not been discovered even though some of the boxes had been removed when the train stopped at Irkutsk.

Peeping through a gap in the pile of boxes, she had watched Nazir Kapoor and his two cronies repeatedly searching up and down the train, looking increasingly irate at not being able to find her. The carriages had a loudspeaker service that announced the approaching stations, so Asha knew exactly when to get off. Better still, the train arrived at Novosibirsk in the dead of night, so she was able to slip out and disappear unnoticed. After that, she just had to endure the seemingly endless journey down through Kazakhstan to Uzbekistan. Asha was relieved to be free from her three pursuers who were still on the Trans-Siberian Express, heading further and further away from her with every passing minute.

In order to get from Samarkand station to the ancient site that once formed the heart of the old city, Asha took a motorised rickshaw. Based on an old-fashioned Fiat car, it chugged and spluttered its way through the crowded streets at little more than walking pace. Even so, she wished her father could have had one of these. He had died young as a result of pulling his human-powered carriage around Kolkata all of his working life. One of these would have saved him so much back-breaking labour. Asha desperately wished he was still here and could know what she was doing. All those hours he had spent giving her a basic education were certainly paying off now.

Asha expected to enjoy her visit to this World Heritage Site, but despite all of the beautiful decorations on the three college buildings, it remained a somewhat sinister and unpleasant place. Right up until the last century, public executions were held at the site. Worse still, the Turkish warlord Tamerlane, relative of the mighty Genghis Khan, displayed his grizzly spoils of war here – the heads of his enemies mounted on spikes. Asha gave a shudder as she learned about this from a tour guide.

As her tour party headed in one direction, Asha sneaked off on her own and went in the other. She wanted to receive the final message from the tigers away from prying eyes. Once again, however, the message did not arrive as expected. The first college, Ulugbek Madrasah, was the oldest and Asha imagined standing in front of it would give her the last set of coordinates. Not so! Nor did the communication occur in front of the second highly-coloured building, the Tilya-Kori Madrasah.

It must be this one, thought Asha, moving on to the Sher-Dor Madrasah, which had been built between 1619 and 1636. Thankfully, the coordinates of her tenth and last destination were telepathically dictated to her twitching hand:

GPS 10

55°45'15.00" N,
37°37'11.97" E

Looking up, Asha soon observed why she had needed to reach this third college building. It had large tiger motifs painted on the brightly coloured walls and her guide book informed her that the name Sher-Dor means 'having tigers.'

'Nice one, guys!' chuckled Asha, giving a double thumbs-up sign in recognition of the tigers' witty choice.

Returning to the noisy streets of modern Samarkand, in another ancient vehicle, Asha felt a sense of elation rising in her body. She had almost done it! She had visited nine far-flung destinations all around Asia and was about to discover the whereabouts of the remaining location. Struggling to press the right buttons on her mobile in the bumpy old car, she clumsily managed to enter the coordinates and discovered that she needed to reach Moscow in order to complete her quest. As she had a ticket allowing her to travel anywhere in Russia, Asha decided to continue using the train to complete this last leg of her quest. All she needed to do was travel north and change back onto the Trans-Siberian line. This would take her straight into Russia's capital.

All would have been well and the youngster

would undoubtedly have gone unnoticed by her pursuers but for one small accident that occurred in Samarkand, on that windy day in early March. Asha reached the station and discovered that the next train did not leave for over two hours. Rather than hang about on the crowded concourse, Asha decided to pass the time by looking for a couple of small presents for Dabeet and Madhuk in the open-air bazaar. She soon found some brightly coloured toy cars that she knew they would love and, hurriedly jerking her purse from her rucksack, she accidentally pulled out her train ticket as well. It was just a thin piece of paper and it quickly blew away, disappearing among all the other litter and rubbish generated by the busy market. At first, Asha was very upset and tried in vain to find her lost ticket. But time was running out and although she hated to waste money, Corinne's credit card was still working, so it was not a problem to get a replacement ticket for the remaining journey back up to Moscow. Hurrying to the station, she bought her final ticket just in time to catch the connecting train she had been waiting for. Habit made her gaze out of the window in search of hostile faces, but there were none.

'After all,' she chuckled to herself, 'those three goons don't know where I am now and there's no way they can find out!'

Asha was quite wrong, of course. Details of her latest credit card purchase instantly went through to Kolkata and were intercepted by Ranjana's father. The bank manager was under strict instructions to pass on vital information like this at any hour of the day or night. So, he relayed it immediately to Nazir Kapoor's mobile phone as the irate father and his two equally frustrated sidekicks sat in a Moscow coffee house, wondering just what they were supposed to do next.

As Asha's train pulled into the station, she was eager to change onto the Trans-Siberian Express and complete the long, tiring journey. As she jumped off the train, Asha turned pale as she was immediately confronted by three menacing figures.

As they stood on the platform waiting for her, the expression on their faces, and the clenched fists and handcuffs in their pockets, meant that this was truly the end of the line for Asha. There was no escaping them this time!

Chapter 10

Bollywood Heroine

Asha sat in the carriage, handcuffed to Dhalia Menokki. She felt very uncomfortable. She had refused to take off any of her outdoor clothes, even though the carriage was heated, so she now felt very hot. She didn't speak and kept her head turned away, pretending to look out of the window, which made her neck ache. So far, her ploys had worked well. Her true identity remained a secret and her three captors had no idea that she was not the real Corinne.

The view from the window was as bleak as Asha's thoughts. The scenery on the east coast had mainly been wide-open fields covered with snow. The views down in Kazakhstan had been of mysterious dark forests, craggy mountains and deep blue lakes. Now, back in industrial west Russia, all Asha could see were roads, houses, factories ... and more snow. It fell all the time, quickly turning brown as it hit the dirty streets and settling around the train window, framing the depressing scene with glitter and sparkle like a picture from a children's book. Oh, how Asha wished she could be back with her family. She was sick of this mission. It had turned into a nightmare and looked like it would end in failure. That was more than she could bear.

What happened next felt like a miracle. As the train entered the outskirts of Moscow, Asha saw a petrol advert on a huge board beside the line. The picture showed a Bengal tiger leaping forwards over a fast-moving car. Whether it was the motion of the train, the swirling snow, Asha's imagination or something far more mysterious, the girl could have sworn she saw the tiger move! It appeared to turn its head on one side in a questioning manner, as if to ask: Is that it? You are giving up?

Suddenly, Asha felt fired up with new resolve. It was a moment often called an epiphany – a split-second when an idea becomes clear and an important decision is reached concerning the future. Asha's epiphany took her waning desire to succeed and turned it into a will of iron. She *would* escape her captors! She *would* succeed in her quest!

Dhalia Menokki noticed the change in Asha by the sudden jerk of the girl's body.

'Sit still!' she barked.

'I need the toilet,' said Asha, quickly.

'You take her, Dhalia,' commanded Nazir Kapoor.

'I'm not going in with her!' exclaimed the woman.

'Just wait outside,' sighed the factory owner, wearily. 'She can't get away.'

'I'll come with you,' added Narmal Vazkar. 'Just in case she tries any funny stuff!'

The handcuffs were unlocked to allow Asha into the cramped toilet. Bolting the door from inside, she gave a sigh of relief at being alone for a moment. Then she looked around for a way of escape. There was none ... or so it seemed. The grey-glassed window was tiny and did not open, so there was no way out through that. But there was a small skylight in the roof! Asha could just reach it by standing on the toilet seat. She felt her heart begin to race with excitement as she pushed it and felt it was not secured.

So, with one hard thump of her fist, she flipped it open like the lid of a metal teapot. Cold air and snowflakes blasted down at her from above, stinging her eyes, but Asha did not care. Was this hole big enough to climb through? Just about – but it was going to be a really tight squeeze!

Taking off her thick coat but retaining her hat and rucksack, Asha thrust her arms up through the hole and then used them to lever herself upwards. At one point, she really thought she was going to get stuck and remain half-in and half-out of the train all the way to Moscow. She imagined herself having to be cut free by firemen, her face frozen stiff and her lips black with frostbite. Somehow, though, she managed to wriggle free and, with one last superhuman effort, heaved herself upwards like a cork popping out of a bottle. She found herself on the roof of the train, shivering with cold and almost blinded by the driving snow. But she was free!

Scrambling along the roof of the speeding train, Asha felt like the heroine of a Bollywood adventure film she had seen as a child. The only difference was that this was for real and one slip would almost certainly end in death. She managed to reach a gap between two of the carriages just before reaching a tunnel that could have sliced off her head. Hanging onto the metal inspection handles, that ran up the sides of the coaches, she managed to wedge herself in a safe but not very comfortable position. How much further was it to Moscow? She did not know. Every minute out in the noisy dark and cold felt like an hour, but every turn of the wheels took her nearer to her final destination.

Before very long, Dhalia Menokki and Narmal Vazkar became suspicious of the long silence from within the toilet and started pounding on the door.

'What's going on?' asked Nazir Kapoor, joining them.

'She's not coming out,' answered Narmal Vazkar.

'Break the door down,' ordered Nazir Kapoor, immediately. It took several shoves by all three of them before the bolt gave way and they fell into the empty toilet in a heap. Asha had thought to replace the trapdoor and jam it tight with her heel, so it appeared she had just vanished into thin air! If this had been a Bollywood film, the baffled expressions on the faces of the villains would have had the whole cinema rocking with laughter.

Just as Asha thought she could hold on no more and would have to jump, probably to her death, the long platforms of Moscow's central station came into view. Gritting her teeth and screwing up her face, she clung on for a few more minutes until the train had almost stopped. Then, before anyone had a chance to get off, she let go and collapsed onto the platform. There was no time to stretch her aching limbs or rub some warmth into her frozen body. She had to get away before anyone spotted her. So, running up the platform as quickly as her stiff legs would allow, Asha thrust her ticket at the startled-looking barrier official and disappeared into the mid-afternoon Moscow crowds like a snowflake melting into a pool.

Her final destination was not far away and Asha made her way through the busy streets on foot, not caring about the strange glances she attracted from passers-by for not wearing a coat. Soon, she arrived at the large paved area in front of the main office of the Russian government. Asha stood right in the centre of the wide open space, turning in all four directions of the compass with her arms held out to show she had reached the final location.

Immediately, she heard the tigers' telepathy talking directly into her mind. The voice said: 'Congratulations, Asha. You have nearly completed your mission. In five minutes' time, we shall dictate a block of letters to you that you must write down. The names of the ten places that you have visited are hidden in this block. None of them are prefixed by the word "the" and many have been split up. All of them are spelt in every direction including backwards. Find them all and cross them out. Then, when you have finished, carefully transfer the remaining letters in order from top to bottom and write them underneath the block. This will tell you exactly where to look for the second Astral Legacy.'

Asha hurried to a quiet corner of this world-famous plaza in the heart of Moscow and sat down with her paper and pen at the ready. Five minutes later to the second, her hand began to twitch and she felt herself writing down a long series of letters in the shape of a grid.

Asha stared at what she had written for a long, long time, unable to make any sense of it at all. She began to panic. What would happen if she couldn't decipher this puzzle? Her whole mission would fail right at the end. Maybe she should ask someone to help her. Nothing was said about having to solve the puzzle on her own. Yes, that was the answer!

She'd stop some passers-by to see if they had any ideas. They'd need to be visitors because the puzzle was not in Russian. She looked around …

'Excuse me, I wonder if you can help me?' called Asha, jumping up and waving her hand as if calling a taxi. Next moment, she realised she had made the greatest mistake of her life. The visitors that Asha had beckoned were Dhalia Menokki, Narmal Vazkar and Nazir Kapoor!

Asha took to her heels once more, but they soon caught up with her. So she played her trump card. Yanking off her hat and shaking her hair free, she revealed who she was.

'I'm Asha Ghosh, not Corinne Kapoor!' she announced.

The faces of her pursuers looked stunned with disbelief. Then all three went white with fury. Nazir Kapoor stepped forwards and grabbed Asha by the throat.

'You've nearly killed us all,' he roared. 'Now we're going to kill you!'

What happens next?

Find the words that make up the ten key locations that Asha visits on her quest in the wordsearch puzzle on page 132. Then carefully transfer the remaining, unused letters in order from top to bottom, left to right and write them in the space provided opposite the wordsearch. This final word is the secret location of the second Astral Legacy. The tigers have provided you with additional clues to help you complete this task on pages 130–31.

When you have worked out the location of the second Astral Legacy log on to www.astrallegacies.com to report the answer. If you successfully enter this final landmark into the website, the adventure is complete and you will be able to read the thrilling climax to *Tigers' Secret* online.

Read the book ... find the hidden locations ... solve the puzzle ... save the world!

www.astrallegacies.com

Addtional Tigers' Clues

PAKISTAN

GPS CODE 1 – A beautiful white marble building in Agra, India. Houses the tombs of an emperor and his wife.

GPS CODE 2 – A minaret without the 't' in Lahore.

GPS CODE 3 – The highest mountain in the world, first climbed by Sir Edmund Hillary and Sherpa Tenzing Norgay.

GPS CODE 4 – Two equal towers which are located in the heart of Colombo's Finance District.

GPS CODE 5 – A volcano in the Sunda Strait between Java and Sumatra, Indonesia.

GPS CODE 6 – The main residence of the emperor of Tokyo, Japan.

GPS CODE 7 – A stone structure thousands of kilometres long, built to protect China from attack.

GPS CODE 8 – Trains stop at Russia's most important Pacific Ocean port.

GPS CODE 9 – The heart of ancient Samarkand with three madrasahs.

GPS CODE 10 – The most famous city square in Moscow, Russia.

Wordsearch

Find and ring all of the words that make up the ten key locations that Asha visits on her quest in the wordsearch. The remaining, unused letters (in order from top to bottom, left to right) make up the location of the second Astral Legacy.

T	A	J	K	R	E	G	I	S	T	A	N
A	V	R	T	S	E	R	E	V	E	C	A
E	E	L	E	R	A	N	I	M	E	E	T
R	S	E	A	M	L	L	L	D	I	N	S
G	O	C	N	D	A	A	A	R	M	T	I
O	U	A	U	R	I	R	Y	H	N	R	K
T	A	L	H	R	T	V	E	U	A	E	A
E	R	A	E	D	L	I	O	D	L	M	P
I	E	P	L	E	S	M	C	S	L	O	C
K	M	R	E	K	R	A	K	A	T	A	U
I	O	G	N	O	I	T	A	T	S	O	G
W	A	L	L	O	F	C	H	I	N	A	K

Location of the Second Astral Legacy

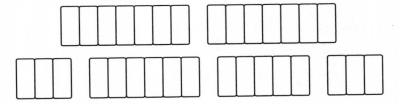

The unused letters from the wordsearch fit perfectly into the boxes above and reveal the location of the second Astral Legacy. When you have worked out the location, log on to www.astrallegacies.com and submit the answer to unlock the thrilling climax to the story. Good luck with your quest!

The Astral Legacies Series

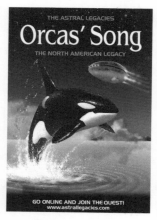

Orcas' Song

The North American Legacy. Book 1

Tigers' Secret

The Asian Legacy. Book 2

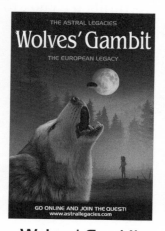

Wolves' Gambit

The European Legacy. Book 3

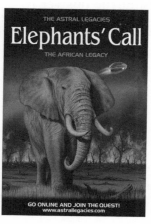

Elephants' Call

The African Legacy. Book 4

The Astral Legacies Series

Condors' Quest
The South American Legacy. Book 5

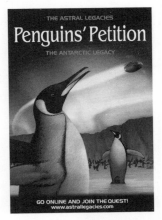

Penguins' Petition
The Antarctic Legacy. Book 6

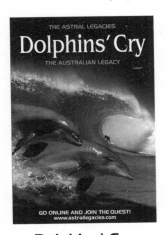

Dolphins' Cry
The Australian Legacy. Book 7

Available from all good bookshops.

Notes

connor R is my
best Buddy ✓✓✓
✓✓✓✓ || ||
well done!
buddy!

C R Rules

C R ROCKS

connor R
is a fun person

Notes

CoR Rules

CoR

CoR ROCKS

Connor.R

is my Best

Buddy

Well done!

Buddy!

About the Author

Gordon Volke's commercial writing career began in 1972 when he was responsible for inventing the comic antics of Dennis the Menace, Minnie the Minx and The Bash Street Kids in the UK's best-selling comic, *The Beano*.

Since this auspicious start to his writing career, Gordon has gained plaudits by originating material for *Snoopy* (*Peanuts*), *Tom and Jerry, Popeye* and *Garfield*, and has been the principal contributor for numerous comics and magazines, including *Twinkle, Thomas the Tank Engine*, *The James Bond Experience* and *Jurassic Park*.

In 1998, Gordon began writing for *The Tweenies*, the Bafta award-winning pre-school series, scripting 44 of the 365 episodes.

Over the years Gordon has originated children's books covering most genres and age categories. He lives near Brighton on the south coast of England.